SAN

Village of du...

Sandsnarl is a settlement steeped in sand –
though where it came from and how long ago
is a matter of tall tales and steely whispers.
The sand itself makes accurate record-keeping
impossible. It is drug, ore, plague and delicacy.
The inhabitants of this region (or is it a fallen
kingdom?) talk and think through its haze.
Some alter their shape, as if shaved by it. Others
seethe, resisting its rattle and buzz.

These poems eavesdrop, extract, sift. Together,
they make up a brief impression of time and
place, a Buñuelian musical without the music.

YES, YES, 100%
yes

SANDSNARL

Poems by Jon Stone
Illustrations by Emma Dai'an Wright

THE EMMA PRESS

First published in the UK in 2021 by the Emma Press Ltd

Text © Jon Stone 2021
Illustrations © Emma Dai'an Wright 2021

ISBN 978-1-912915-79-8

A CIP catalogue record of this book
is available from the British Library.

Printed and bound in the UK
by the Holodeck, Birmingham.

The Emma Press
theemmapress.com
hello@theemmapress.com
Jewellery Quarter, Birmingham, UK

Supported using public funding by
ARTS COUNCIL
ENGLAND
LOTTERY FUNDED

CONTENTS

"These mind things are very strong; in some, so strong as to blot out the external things completely."

John Steinbeck, The Log from the *Sea of Cortez*

The Thulr of Sand, Whose Mouth Hovers Eternally Above a Cup of Mead, Orates the Beginnings of the Age of Sand

Before there was a now, there was a jar.
The jar contained a sandstorm, an infinitude of sand
that twined and tore, intensely muscular
and infinitely busy in the enterprise of sand.

It lingered in a storeroom, on a lip
of shelf behind some milk crates, a small and secret thing,
till someone missed their step or lost their grip,
delivering a tremor that impelled a teetering.

The floor came up, and what was in that jar
went reeling and unrealing over all that ever was.
Sand. Not gravel, clay or silty tar.
No hoggin, pebble, cobble, soil or granite dust for us.

Every road and jitty, copse and field,
the squares and public gardens – all were avalanched in sand.
The breweries were jammed. The ponds were filled.
The market stalls and fairs – dishevelled, overrun with sand.

houses, as in churches and hotels,
teacups, as in ovens, as in pantries: drifts of sand.
e drank and cooked amongst its particles.
e suffered it. We slept with it. We breathed and bathed in sand.

blowed and scurried through our ears, our heads,
covering the whole of us, then hiding it again.
nd amid our folds, our fresh bedspreads,
fingers on our decks, doing its shuffle-hurricane.

blurred our plans. It blurred the names on stones.
e border between sand and dream became a spit of sand.
choked our clocks. It doped our pheromones.
ery book we owned became *Miscellany of Sand.*

d now we mine the sand beneath the sand.
e shovel sand – we feed it into furnaces of sand.
e pray for sand, and lay the blame on sand.
all my daughter, Sand. I call my other daughter, Sand.

The Drysalter of Sand Presses His Lips to Your Ear and Rehearses, or Rather Rasps, His Summer Catalogue

A bottle of weed-green Olivine sand from Norway:
pour into bathwater. Store in a drawer, or nowhere.
A phial of coral and limestone sand from Hawaii
to douse a device that is wayward, on fire, or haywire.
A jug of plum sand from Pfeiffer Beach in Australia:
open, then leave it to breathe beneath rampant starlight.
A pyxis or two of basaltic sand, ash-slack and Cretan:
portion out cautiously over a breakfast encounter.
An olla of skeleton sand from an island off Venice:
stow with your souvenirs, or with your ice or fine silver.
A magnum of magnetite sand from Barbados – no, Bali:
empty the lot on the tarmac at night, in a lay-by.
An ampoule of impure and volatile sand from Dorset
to rub in the eye of your wound every time you undress it.

A Smuggler, Pursued Across the Shore in a Cloud of Sand-fog, Divests Himself of the Evidence that Would Convict Him

He hurls his bag beyond a slanted fence.
It gasps its turbulence of grains – unburnished, blonde –
into a wondrous wind of much the same.

He rifles through his nights alone in bed,
to strip away their medley of volcanic contraband.
He brushes candied remnants from his flame.

He empties out his breast, his pit, his will.
He shakes the fragrant silica from every little gape.
He stoops to scrape his skull clean, then his name.

The Roboteer Hesitates on the Cusp, Before Easing Herself At Last into the Cab of Her Golem

Gently quaking,
her flight suit a half-sloughed snakeskin,
she sinks amid cables and instrumentation.

This is her girl,
this poor machine, once agile,
whose radiator now begins to gurgle.

Sand in the intakes.
Sand in the joins of panels and joysticks,
crackling as she runs preliminary diagnostics.

Then each raises
the other's stiff engine from its stasis.
Her fingers dance across gamuts of indicators.

Heat, and a hum
to hold the pair in equilibrium.
She wears her summoned sweat like healing balm.

But what are we to do about
the Sand Weasels? You don't
know them? I will explain:

The sand weasels' ploy
is to be but one boy
   in the derelict light,
and a wild nest of imps
at the third or fourth glimpse,
   quicksilver, slight.

Their busy, bronze pelts
shock the sun, as they pulse
   with exuberance.
They are messily quiffed
and they easily drift
   in and out of their pants.

And the boy that they are
is his own avatar,
   his own spoilt prince.
In the woods, after nightfall,
when the wind's not so spiteful
   he strikes his flints.

Racked and Red-Eyed in a Sad Scrag of Waistcoat, The Sandsinger Tells Why His Concerts Are Cancelled

There was a note I couldn't seem to reach,
a note I'd stumbled on – this briny tune
had washed up in my heart and made an itch.
I tried a line in bass, then baritone,
and maybe half way through I felt the catch,
I sung that snag, that fragment of a groan.

Not too high, no, not too low – it just
existed in a cleft within my range.
A grain that did not melt, would not be crushed,
and which I could not shape, dissolve, expunge.
In fact, the more I played the alchemist
the more it seemed to fatten in revenge.

It multiplied. Its clones advanced beyond
the limits of the verse. Oh, they were clever;
they hid in jingles, oddball ditties, spawned
discreetly. Then they overran my oeuvre,
and soon I couldn't cover up the wound –
my throat was torn. I was myself a sliver.

The note has birthed a pentatonic scale;
entire folk traditions now draw from it,
whose adherents hold sway in every school.
My star can only sputter now, then plummet.
My destiny is to be miniscule,
the village sot, the caterwauling hermit.

Things the Sand Orphan Mumbles, Half to Himself and Half to His Distant Darling, as He Journeys Upward and Out of the Underground Station

The way I tow your shadow like a tugboat.
The way I fade beneath it as I tow.

The way my triumph seems so long ago
I could be Eadwig, Æthelwulf or Ecgberht.

The way the walls are plastered with my mugshot
because of what you know I know you know.

The way one look behind me ends the show,
despite our story being mere subplot.

The way my body burbles like a dovecot,
with birds it wants to loose into the snow.

The way this staircase seems to grow and grow.
The way I play my bit-part as the cutthroat.

The way I did the things I did for love, but
got caught up in the mutant afterglow.

An Argument About Sand

It's ballast, says the almoner, pure ballast.
It weighs upon our sacks of self, preventing
too much lamenting.
The lightshipman, whose hands are broad and callused,
dissents, insists its purpose is to tutor
us on our future.

And all is uproar, all disquiet; none of the rest of them buy

The crucial thing about it is its skitter,
avers the weaver, since it makes us listen
for each admission.
No, no, no, no, the locksmith begs to differ,
the point is that it fills the crannies we can't,
the nooks left vacant.

And all is turmoil, all disquiet; none of the rest of them buy

What matters is it's ours, suggests the doctor.
What matters is that most of it is no one's,
the brightsmith motions.
It's like a rudeness one keeps in one's sock drawer
but at the same time flashes at the jealous,
attests the cellist.

And all is furore, all commotion,
since that one at least was a close one.

Attempts to Describe One Who Lived Here, and Who May Have Been a Ghost or a Djinn or an Extraordinary Feature of the Weather

Tearaway. Huckster. Familiar. Stray.
Luminous plasma. Perpetual affray.
Innocent. Inner light. In on the con.
Whatever she was, she's gone.

Tremor of headlamp. Fugitive purr.
Snag in the wrinkle of signature
that sits on a pseudepigraphon.
Whatever she was, she's gone, boys. She's gone.

Sand cat. Coyote. Tarantula. Mole.
Spy for the old foe, or central control,
sent to foreshadow the dénouement.
Whatever she was, she's gone.

Fata morgana, or siren, or sphinx.
Last of the glamour through which the hag slinks.
Mask someone wore with a will of its own.
Whatever she was, she's gone, boys. Gone.

The Travelling Tea Seller Has Laid Out Their Stall Beneath a Willow Tree and is Entertaining Their First Customer

This. Now, this – inhale its pretty whiff.
A puzzle, yes? A nasal logograph.
All down to how it's picked and dried. The thief
who fled her city with it says its
leaves are rolled on the exquisite,
sand-encrusted thighs of a naïf.

Or was it 'waif'? Or 'novice'? I forget.
In any case, this young initiate
then cures them in the salt of their own sweat,
which is collected through their efforts
at – I can't remember if it's
sport or pleasuring some baronet.

Said baronet – I may mean 'duke' or 'knight' –
is known to have a ranging appetite.
So says my thief, who was his acolyte.
And more, I think, to judge by how her
eyes flamed and her look turned sour –
Ah? You'll take the lot. I thought you might.

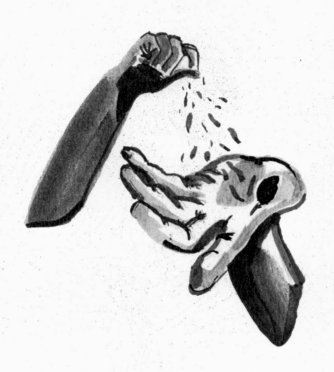

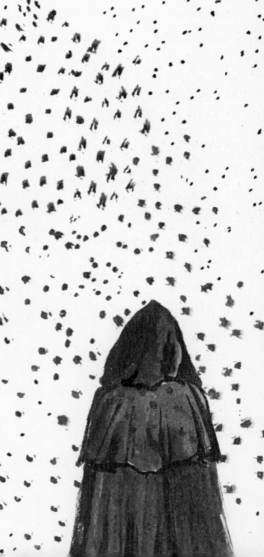

The Scandal-Mired Sandskinshifter, on Learning That She is Not on the Guest List for a Certain Party, Prepares Her Disguise

I will wear the meat-sock body of a cheetah
and saunter greedily, leggily,

in through the foyer as if going to the theatre,
like one louche gunslinger trailing another

through town and prairie to Deadgoon Gully,
and fling the dust-sheet off the evening's throne

when I usher, gaily,
my cat-self's swaying bridge (tail a frayed tether)

over the threshold, the indisputable honcho
of the gala,

and don as raiments, as regalia
the ensuing panoply of panic,

before I pause beneath the pergola,
reclining in my own cat-gaze, very languishing,

a living chaise longue.

Two Makers of Sand Toys, Both Skilled and Ancient, Disconcerted and Dark-Browed, Open Their Doors for Business at the Same Hour on the Same Side-street

The things they sell are intricate;
each glassy micro-cabinet
has dials and pivots,
pegs and spinners,
small, articulated figures
which the dyed sands animate
as they pour and percolate.
Vignettes, folk scenes,
dances, mazes –
some are visual fantasias,
castle, sea or woodland-themed,
filigreed or pewter-rimmed.
But ask one craftsman
then the other
what they're for and what they further.

One talks low, of fates and spells
and thralls and charms and not much else,
and looks triumphant,
while his rival
says, as if in cold reprisal
(tight-jawed, tense), that each exists
to make you guess why it exists,
then reels his breath in.
Damned fool question.

An Explosion at the Plant Nearly Tears the Sky from its Moorings

Some of us consider it well-timed.
We drink its radiance through windows rimed
with quiet expectation, eyes abloom.

Some of us are swearing vengeance on
whichever natural phenomenon,
or cult, or loner raised the roaring plume.

Some of us are sure it's all a ruse.
As sand begins to rain down on our roofs,
we turn back to our drinks. We pace and fume.

Some of us believe the facts we fudged
have turned up in some book, that we are judged.
We hug our broken toys and quit the room.

The Heretic Limnologist Produces an Underground Pamphlet Expounding on the Dreaming of Rivers, and it Says

that river-dreams unravel when they catch on sunken metalwork,
at sites of ancient moorings, say, where scattered on the riverbed
are shots of chain, and here and there the furred tusk of an anchor fluke;

that river-dreams are chains that slip into the high tide of the head,
that load us with their links and drag us down toward the riverbank,
our brains made into monkeyfists, our hearts all smeared with river mud;

that river-dreams are formed from foam that gathers at the river's flank,
eventually congealing into stories, songs and monologues
which document the river's mood, the river's blood, the river's stink;

that river-dreams are rotted through, their flesh a spoil of river-slugs,
are hooked and netted, then tossed back, or passed round to provoke disgust,
are swallowed whole and swallow what has swallowed them, from lungs to lugs;

that river-dreams are things we ought to tag and track, dissect, discuss,
that each one is a flensing knife, a double bluff, a brittle spark.
(The heretic limnologist is still at large and dangerous.)

The Elderly Astronomer Sits in What Wa
Once the Churchyard, Reading (so She is
Given to Understand) a Long-Lost Nove
George Sand

And as she turns a page, intent on knowing what comes n
the cars of the police start to arrive.

They close their doors so tenderly. They straighten out their
Sand runs from her sleeve.

ACKNOWLEDGEMENTS

Thanks to: Borges for writing his *Book of Sand*. It Calvino for leaving behind a *Collection of Sand*. Nick Dr for tailoring his 'Clothes of Sand'. Inspector Imani for searching through the *Castle of Sand*. Al Stewart putting *Sand in Your Shoes*.

And to: *The Rialto* for sheltering the Heretic Limnolog Kirsten Irving, Kate Potts, Holly Hopkins, Angela Clel and Alison Winch for editorial input (and friendship).

And to Emma Wright for her brilliant work bring *Sandsnarl* to life.

ABOUT THE POET

Stone is a Derbyshire-born writer, editor and
earcher. He won an Eric Gregory Award in 2012 and
Poetry London Prize in 2014 and 2016. *School of
gery* (Salt, 2012) was chosen as a Poetry Book Society
commendation. He designs and edits collaborative
xed media anthologies with Sidekick Books and has a
D in poem-videogame interplay.

w.gojonstonego.com

ABOUT THE ILLUSTRATOR

1ma Dai'an Wright is a British-Chinese-Vietnamese
blisher and illustrator based in Birmingham.

The Emma Press

small press, big dreams

The Emma Press is an independent publisher dedicated to producing beautiful, thought-provoking books. It was founded in 2012 by Emma Dai'an Wright in Winnersh, UK, and is now based in Birmingham.

The Emma Press has been shortlisted for the Michael Marks Award for Poetry Pamphlet Publishers in 2014, 2015, 2016, 2018 and 2020, winning in 2016.

In 2020 The Emma Press was awarded funding from Arts Council England as part of the Elevate programme.

The Emma Press publishes themed poetry anthologies, single-author poetry and fiction chapbooks and books for children, with a growing list of translations.

The Emma Press is passionate about publishing literature which is welcoming and accessible. Sign up to the Emma Press newsletter to hear about upcoming events, publications and calls for submissions.

theemmapress.com